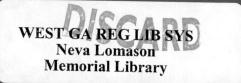

NIGHT OF THE LIVING GERBIL

NIGHT OF THE LIVING GERBIL

ELIZABETH LEVY

ILLUSTRATED BY
BILL BASSO

HarperCollinsPublishers

Library of Congress Cataloging-in-Publication Data
Levy, Elizabeth.
     Night of the living gerbil / Elizabeth Levy ; illustrated by
Bill Basso.
         p.   cm.
     Summary: Sam and his brother, Robert, fear their new
neighbor is a zombie and plans to bring their dead pet gerbil
back to life.
     ISBN 0-06-028588-5 — ISBN 0-06-028589-3 (lib. bdg.)
     [1. Brothers—Fiction. 2. Gerbils—Fiction. 3. Pets—
Fiction. 4. Death—Fiction.] I. Basso, Bill, ill. II. Title.
PZ7.L5827 Nl 2001   00-054230
[Fic]—dc21   CIP
                                                      AC

Typography by Andrea Simkowski
1 3 5 7 9 10 8 6 4 2
❖
First Edition

To Gingey—Biting toes up in heaven

CONTENTS

NIGHT OF THE
LIVING GERBIL

1

READY FOR THE REAL EXTERMINATOR

"Look at Extermie," shouted Robert to his brother, Sam, one Saturday morning. "I think there's something wrong with him."

Robert had two gerbils, Terminator and Exterminator—called Termie and Extermie for short. Termie was playing on the wheel in their cage, making it go around and around. But Extermie was lying on the bottom of the cage, his little back legs splayed out behind him.

Robert picked up the cage and carried it to Sam's room to show him. Sam was busy on the computer. He barely looked up. "Maybe he's ready for the real exterminator," he joked. "You know—the one who comes to the apartment and sprays for cockroaches. Maybe you tempted fate giving him that name."

"That's not funny," said Robert. He took Extermie out of the cage and stroked his head gently. Extermie just lay there. His little chest went up and down with each breath, but he didn't tickle Robert's palm with his claws like he usually did.

Robert carried Extermie over to Sam. "Do you really think it was a mistake to name him Exterminator?" he asked.

Sam finally looked up from the computer and stared at the gerbil cradled in his brother's hands. Extermie's eyes did look a little glassy. "Maybe we should show him to Mom," Sam suggested. He was starting to feel a little guilty about his joke.

Mrs. Bamford was sitting at the kitchen counter, surrounded by pieces of paper. "I need a science program!" she muttered without looking up. "It's got to be perfect."

Sam and Robert glanced at each other. Mrs. Bamford was in charge of cultural

programs for Sam and Robert's school this year, and she was determined to do the best job ever. But her first two assemblies had not been great successes.

First, she had booked "To Be or Not to Be Shakespeare," an acting troupe that promised to perform one scene from each of Shakespeare's plays in a hilarious, fun-filled forty-five-minute assembly. Unfortunately, two hours after they started, the troupe hadn't even gotten to act one of *Hamlet*. Most of the kids were asleep. The ones who weren't were throwing spitballs at each other.

Then Mrs. Bamford had set up an author appearance. But the visiting author had just broken his leg, and he spent the entire assembly having kids write jokes on his cast. He also told a lot of jokes. At least some of them were about writing—

"How do you begin a book about ducks?"

"With an intro-duck-tion."

"How does a book about zombies begin?"

"With a 'dead-ication.'"

The kids had fun, but the teachers told

Mrs. Bamford that they weren't sure it had been a true learning experience.

Now Mrs. Bamford had just enough money left from the Parent Teacher Organization to do one last program. She wanted it to be a good one and had decided that a science program was the way to go.

"Mom, Exterminator isn't feeling well," said Robert.

Mrs. Bamford peered at Robert's gerbil. "He does look a little peaked."

"He's sleeping a lot more than Termie, and I think he's losing weight," said Robert.

"Yup," said Sam. "Looks like he's ready for that last ride in the compactor chute to the sky."

"Shut up," said Robert, covering Extermie's ears. "You're upsetting him."

"He doesn't want to know what happens to New York City pets when they go belly up," teased Sam. "Remember what happened to Goldie?"

"I don't want to talk about Goldie," said Robert.

Goldie, Robert's first pet, had been a

goldfish. He had ended up being flushed down the toilet. Sam was the one who had done the flushing.

"How about cute little Gravy Crockett?" asked Sam.

Gravy Crockett, Robert's second pet, had been a turtle. He had only lasted a few weeks. And then he had died. Mrs. Bamford had wrapped him up and put him down the apartment's garbage chute to the basement compactor. It was a good thing it happened on a day that the garbage was picked up, as Mrs. Bamford pointed out.

Then Robert had gotten Terminator and Exterminator. He had had them for a whole six months so far, and they were his favorite pets of all. They were furry, sweet, and, despite their names, they never destroyed anything except a little bit of newspaper.

"Mom, I think we should take Extermie to the vet," said Robert.

Mrs. Bamford nodded. "We'll take a taxi. It'll be quicker."

Robert wrapped Extermie up in a clean towel and put him in his carrying case. Sam helped. He was feeling a little bad about the jokes he had made. Sometimes he just couldn't help himself. But he didn't want Extermie to die.

2

WEIRD SCIENCE

At the animal clinic, Dr. Simon unwrapped the towel that Robert had wrapped Extermie in and peered at him closely for several seconds. Then he shook his head.

"Please don't do that," Robert begged.

"Do what?" asked Dr. Simon.

"You shook your head," explained Sam. "Kind of like there's no hope."

"I'm sorry, Robert," said Dr. Simon. "But it doesn't look very good."

Robert looked up at his mother with tears in his eyes.

"Isn't there anything you can do?" Mrs. Bamford asked.

"Well, I can try giving him fluids, but there's really not a lot I can—" Dr. Simon paused, looking down at Robert's stricken face. "Why don't you leave him here overnight. You can find out how he is in the morning."

Sam had a feeling that in the morning the news would not be good. Robert must have thought so too. He walked out of the vet's office with his head down.

As they started to walk to the subway, they passed Weird Science, a store that sold all sorts of fossils and bones. It had only been open a few weeks, but Sam had already visited it half a dozen times.

"Let's go in," suggested Sam. He thought it could be the perfect place to help Robert take his mind off Extermie.

"I don't feel like it," said Robert.

"Come on. It'll cheer you up," urged Sam, glancing at their mother. "Mom, don't you think Robert needs cheering up?"

"We'll go in for just a minute," said Mrs. Bamford.

Some stores have a bell or a buzzer that goes off when a customer walks in. But at

Weird Science, when the door opened, an elephant's bellow sounded. Mrs. Bamford jumped. Sam just grinned.

"Be with you in a minute," said a pale, thin man dressed in a safari jacket and jeans. He was bent over the counter, working on something that seemed to involve a bunch of very small bones.

The man looked up and recognized Sam. "Oh, hello Sam." He smiled. He had a gold cap on one tooth. Most of his hair was marching backward from his forehead, but what hair he had left was streaked with gray, and he wore it long, pulled back in a ponytail.

"Hi, Mr. Winston," said Sam. "Mom, this is Mr. Winston. He's the owner. Mr. Winston, this is my mom and my little brother, Robert."

Robert didn't like being introduced as the little brother, even if it was true. He looked around. Sam had told him how cool this store was, but now that he was here, he didn't like it. It smelled. A very strange smell—kind of like a combination of a zoo and a chemistry set.

Mr. Winston smiled at Mrs. Bamford. "You must have another name besides Mom."

Mrs. Bamford laughed. "Sometimes I wonder . . . I'm Karen Bamford."

"I'm Ben," said Mr. Winston. "May I call you Karen?"

"Please do," said Mrs. Bamford.

Sam shifted his weight from one foot to the other. He was having second thoughts. Maybe bringing Robert into Weird Science wasn't such a good idea. He had forgotten how many dead animals there were hanging on the walls.

Mrs. Bamford seemed happy to stay awhile. "You really do have some amazing things here, Ben. You know, I always thought of hunting trophies as ugly, but I have to admit that most of these are beautiful."

"Oh, taxidermy is an art form," said Mr. Winston. "At least, I like to think of it that way. Some of these I worked on myself. For example—" He was interrupted by a loud sniffle from Robert. "What's wrong, son?" he asked.

"My gerbil . . . he's . . . he's . . . ," stammered Robert. He couldn't say anything more.

"Robert's gerbil is one step away from

joining the jolly big exterminator in the sky," Sam blurted out.

Robert gasped.

"I'm sorry," said Sam. "That just slipped out. Honest." Sam swallowed hard. He knew the joke was awful, and he wished he could take it back.

Mrs. Bamford gave Sam a warning look. "My son Robert is upset today," she explained to Mr. Winston.

Robert gingerly picked up a stuffed woodchuck. He stared at its little face. Its glassy eyes stared back at him. It looked so real that the whiskers looked ready to twitch. "Was it once alive?" Robert asked in a shaky voice.

"Yes, he was," said Mr. Winston. "And I like to think that I helped make him live again. That's what taxidermy is."

"Extermie hates taxis," sobbed Robert. "He knows it means that he's going to the vet's."

"No, not that kind of taxi," said Mr. Winston. "Taxidermy is the art of preserving animals in their most lifelike form. My grandfather taught my brother and me how

to do it. He would laugh if he heard me, but I think he was an artist, and he taught my brother and me to be artists too. You can see lots of examples of our work in museums of natural history around the country."

"See, Mom," said Sam proudly. "This is like going to an art gallery, but way cooler."

Mrs. Bamford laughed. "I'm always trying to get Sam and Robert to go to museums with me," she explained to Mr. Winston.

"Well, I like to think of my store as a little museum."

"It *is* very interesting," said Mrs. Bamford.

Robert was still stroking the woodchuck that he held in his hands. "He looks so real," he said.

"Well, he *is* real," said Mr. Winston. "My grandpa always said you can't do the work unless you remember that the animal was once as alive as you or me. You've got to respect the animal you're working on. Like right now I'm doing a dead duck." He waggled his eyebrows at Mrs. Bamford.

"Why a duck?" asked Mrs. Bamford, giggling.

14

Sam and Robert stared at their mother. There was nothing really funny about a dead duck.

Then Mr. Winston did something very, very weird. He pretended to flick the ash from the end of a cigar and wagged his eyebrows even more. "Why a duck?" he repeated.

Mrs. Bamford laughed out loud.

"I don't get it," said Sam.

Mr. Winston and Mrs. Bamford smiled at each other.

"It's just a joke from an old Marx Brothers movie," said Mrs. Bamford. "If you say 'why a duck' fast it sounds like 'viaduct'—you know, the bridges the Romans built to carry water."

"It's not a very good joke," said Sam, rolling his eyes.

Mr. Winston grinned at Mrs. Bamford and again pretended to waggle his eyebrows at her.

Sam noticed that he had strange eyebrows that met in a peak—and when he made them go up and down, they looked extremely odd.

"Your mom and I have a lot in common," Mr. Winston said. "We both love Marx Brothers movies."

Mrs. Bamford looked around the shop. "The more I look at the trophies you have here, the more I realize how fascinating they are."

"Oh, don't think of these animals as trophies," said Mr. Winston. "I want people to remember that each of my creations was once a magnificent living creature—as are all God's animals."

"I never thought of it that way," said Mrs. Bamford.

"Hey, Mom—you should have Mr. Winston for your science program," said Sam.

"What a good idea, Sam. Do you ever visit schools, Ben?" asked Mrs. Bamford.

"All the time, Karen. I give talks at natural history museums around the country. I'm always talking to kids."

"What could be cooler than weird science, Mom," said Sam.

"I know what would be cooler," said Robert, putting the woodchuck back on the

16

counter. "The coolest thing would be a miracle for my sick gerbil."

"I wish your gerbil the best," said Mr. Winston.

Mrs. Bamford looked at Mr. Winston gratefully. He really seemed like a nice man. "You know," she said, "I think you would be just the person to have for the science assembly. May I have a business card?"

"Certainly." Mr. Winston handed her a card. "Sam has been a regular customer since we opened. He's such a polite young boy, I just knew his mother must be terrific too."

"Thank you," said Mrs. Bamford.

"And is your husband interested in fossils? Is that where Sam got his curiosity?"

"Uh, I don't think so. We're divorced. He lives in Chicago."

Mr. Winston smiled. "Maybe you could give me your number," he said. "I could call you with some ideas about the science assembly, Karen."

"Thank you, Ben," said Mrs. Bamford.

Robert looked from one to the other. They

sure were using each other's first names a lot. It sounded strange. There was a lot weird about Mr. Winston, and Robert wasn't sure that it all had to do with science.

3

DWIGHT OF THE LIVING DEAD

On Sunday morning, Mrs. Bamford told Sam and Robert that she had to go out for brunch. "Willie will be here soon to baby-sit. And Mabel's coming over to play with you today."

Mrs. Bamford saw the look Sam and Robert gave each other when she mentioned Mabel. "Be nice to her," she warned.

Mabel was Sam and Robert's cousin. She was Robert's age. Or, to be exact, which Mabel often was, she was exactly one week older than Robert. But she acted more grown-up than any other seven-year-old they had ever met. On top of that, she was extremely bossy.

"Why doesn't someone tell Mabel to be nice to me?" complained Sam. "She's always telling me that everything I do is wrong."

"Well, Mabel just has a very highly developed sense of right and wrong," said Mrs. Bamford. She was putting on lipstick and making that funny face she always did when she put it on.

Sam thought there was something a little different about Mrs. Bamford this morning, but he couldn't figure out what it was.

Willie came down around noon. "You smell nice, Mrs. Bamford," he said as she checked herself in the mirror one more time on the way out.

"Thanks, Willie." She gave Willie a beaming smile as if he had just given her the best compliment in the world.

"That must be it," Sam said to her. "You smell different. I knew something was different about you."

Mrs. Bamford smiled and blew a kiss as she left the apartment.

"Your mom looks cool," said Willie when she was gone.

Sam wasn't sure whether he liked Willie calling his mom cool, even though he liked Willie a lot. Sam and Robert had known Willie all their lives. He lived in the same apartment building.

Mabel's parents dropped her off soon after Mrs. Bamford had left.

"Are you joining Mom for brunch?" Sam asked his aunt and uncle.

"No, we're going to the opera this afternoon," said Mabel's mother. "But we'll probably meet them—um . . . her—later."

"Hmmm," said Mabel. She nodded at Sam and Robert as if she knew a secret and they didn't.

Just the way she said "hmmm" annoyed Sam. But a lot that Mabel did annoyed him. For example, she always liked to dress in one color. Most days, she wore grape purple or pumpkin orange. Today, it wasn't even a color. White isn't officially a color, and Mabel was dressed head to toe in white—crisp white jeans, a white T-shirt, and white sneakers without a spot on them.

"Mabel," said Willie, "you're quite dazzling

21

today." He pretended to shield his eyes from the glare.

"I think you look like a hospital nurse," said Sam.

"Don't talk about hospitals," said Robert. He was not in a good mood. They still hadn't heard from Dr. Simon.

Mabel's eyes grew wide. "Why not? Is someone sick?"

"It's Extermie," said Sam. "He's at the vet's. It doesn't look good."

"Oh, Robert, I'm so sorry," said Mabel.

"It's awful," said Robert. "And Sam keeps making sick jokes. Yesterday he reminded me of the time he flushed Goldie down the toilet—and then the time Mom had to put my turtle down the compactor chute."

"The next one we're going to slingshot off the roof," joked Sam.

Willie laughed.

"Shame on you, Sam," said Mabel. "I know about the grief of a pet passing to the other side."

Sam had forgotten that Mabel's guinea pig, Madeline, had died a couple of months ago. Now he felt guiltier than ever about the jokes that kept slipping out of his mouth.

"Hey, Willie," said Sam. "Got any knock-knock jokes?" He figured it was a good time to change the subject. Willie always had great jokes.

"Here's one I just made up after seeing this super movie last night," said Willie. "It's about a guy who can't say words starting with 'n.' When he tries to say 'knock, knock,' it comes out 'dnock, dnock.'"

Robert and Sam giggled.

Mabel frowned. "It's not nice to make fun of speech impediments," she said.

Willie ignored her. "Dnock, dnock," he said.

"Who's there?" asked Sam and Robert together.

"Dwight," said Willie.

"Dwight who?" asked Sam, Robert, and Mabel together.

"Dwight of the living dead," said Willie, cracking up.

Robert's shoulders slumped. Sam wished that Willie had thought of a joke that didn't have the word "dead" in it.

"I don't get it," said Mabel.

Willie didn't seem to notice that Robert was upset. "Haven't you ever seen *Night of the Living Dead*? I rented it last night. It's really scary. It starts off with this brother and sister—they're driving into a graveyard. Everything is fine until they run into a man with long gray hair. He looks normal, but it turns out he's a zombie and so are half the people in town. They have to hide in a house, but they don't know who's a zombie and who's not. You can't tell if someone's alive or one of the living dead. It could be your friend. It could be anybody."

"That doesn't sound so bad," said Robert. "It would be nice if animals or people didn't really have to die. Then if you missed somebody they wouldn't be really gone."

"Be careful what you wish for," said Willie in a scary voice. "In the movie, the dead come back and eat the living."

"I think we should find something else to talk about," said Mabel. "Especially in this, the hour of Robert's anxiety. The possible loss of a gerbil is a very sad thing."

"He's not lost yet," said Robert angrily.

Just then the phone rang. Sam picked it up.

"Hello, this is Dr. Simon. Is your mother there?"

"No, she's not," said Sam.

Sam heard Dr. Simon sigh. "Who am I talking to?" he asked.

"It's Sam."

"Well, I'm afraid I have bad news for your brother," said Dr. Simon. "Is there an adult around that I can talk to?"

Sam looked at Willie. "Well, my next-door neighbor is baby-sitting. He's fourteen."

"I think you'd better put him on the phone," said Dr. Simon.

Sam handed the phone to Willie.

Willie listened. His eyes got wide. He hung up.

"What was that?" asked Robert.

"Uh, nothing," said Willie. "Sam, can I talk to you in your room for a minute?"

Robert's eyes were big. "What's wrong?" he demanded. "Tell me."

"I just need a minute with Sam," said Willie. "We'll be right out."

Robert knew that it was not good news.

THE GERBIL
IS ON THE ROOF

Willie closed the door to Sam's room. "You know that was Dr. Simon on the phone, don't you?" said Willie.

"Extermie's dead, isn't he?" Sam asked.

Willie nodded. "What do you think we should do?"

Sam wished that Willie hadn't asked him. He really didn't know what to do. "Robert knows that something is up," he said. "We'll have to tell him."

"I know," said Willie. He paced around the room. "I'm just trying to figure out the right way to break the news to him. It's got to be done right."

Sam nodded.

Willie bit his lip. "I heard a story once. Well, it's kind of a joke, but . . . listen—tell me if you think it's the way to go. A guy was taking care of his friend's cat. And while the friend was away, the cat died. When the friend came home, the guy who was cat-sitting blurted out, 'Your cat died.'

"The friend was really upset. He said to the guy, 'You should have broken it to me gently. You should have said the cat got out . . . then it got on the roof . . . then we called the fire department . . . and finally the cat fell off the roof.'"

"Why did he want to hear all that if it wasn't true?" asked Sam.

"See, that would have given him time to get used to it," Willie explained. "So the next summer, the man's friend went away again, and he asked the guy to take care of his dog. And the same thing happened. The dog died. But this time, when his friend came home, the guy said, 'Your dog is on the roof.'"

Sam blinked.

"Get it?" asked Willie. "He was warning him that something bad had happened so he'd have time to get used to it."

"You mean we should tell Robert his gerbil is on the roof?" asked Sam.

"Well, it's better than just blurting it out to him," said Willie.

Sam thought about it. He supposed that was true.

Before Willie and Sam could decide what to do, Robert barged into the room, followed by Mabel.

"What are you two talking about?" Robert asked. He sounded upset.

"Uh . . . that was Dr. Simon," said Sam.

"I thought so," said Robert. "I could tell by the way you sounded. What did he have to say?"

"Uh . . . ," Sam began. He wished there *was* a way to tell Robert gently. He glanced at Willie, but Willie was biting his fingernail and looking at the floor. Finally Sam blurted out, "Dr. Simon called and said your gerbil was on the roof." Then he started giggling. He didn't know why he was giggling; he just couldn't stop himself.

"What do you mean, my gerbil was on the roof?" Robert looked shocked.

Sam felt really bad. "Uh . . . Robert—

he's . . ." He couldn't get any words out. His voice was coming out all high and squeaky—kind of like a gerbil's.

"Robert," said Willie, stepping in, "your gerbil isn't really on any roof. That's just a joke. But it's not a joke what happened to Extermie. I'm afraid Dr. Simon was calling with bad news."

"He's dead, isn't he? And you two are making jokes!" said Mabel angrily.

"I thought he was probably dead from the way you looked when you answered the phone," Robert said to Sam. "And then as soon as Willie said that he had to talk to you alone I knew."

"Oh, Robert," said Mabel, throwing her arms around him. "I'm so sorry. I know what you're going through. You need to cry." She forced Robert's head onto her shoulder.

Sam blinked. He kind of wanted to put his arms around his brother too, but Mabel had gotten there first. "I loved Extermie too," said Sam.

Mabel gave Sam a dirty look. "You have a funny way of showing it."

Robert sniffled. But he didn't cry. He just

pressed his lips together tightly and didn't say a word. He didn't even try to free himself from Mabel's clutches. That *really* worried Sam.

Mabel hugged him even tighter. "Robert, do you think you want a funeral service for Extermie?"

"You mean, before Sam flushes him or puts him down the compactor?" asked Robert furiously.

"That's right, get angry, Robert," said Mabel. "Anger is one of the stages of grief. You're doing really well."

"Mabel, what are you talking about?" Sam demanded.

"I know about these things," said Mabel huffily. "I've been through this with Madeline. And Sam Bamford, as I recall, you weren't much comfort."

Sam felt helpless. "Maybe we should call Mom."

"Good idea," said Willie.

They called Mrs. Bamford on her cell phone and told her the news. She asked to speak to Robert.

"Oh Robert," she said. "I'm so sorry about Extermie."

"It's no big deal," muttered Robert. "He's just a gerbil. I don't want to talk about it."

"Shock and denial," whispered Mabel sagely. "Those are the first stages of grief."

Robert handed the phone back to Sam.

Sam got back on and whispered into the phone. "Mom, what should I do?"

"Hold on a moment," said Mrs. Bamford.

Sam heard murmurs in the background and wondered who she was talking to.

Mrs. Bamford got back on the phone. "Instead of meeting you at home, I think I should meet you at the vet's office," she said. "We can decide what to do from there. Tell Willie to take you all over there on the subway. That'll give me time to get there."

"Okay, Mom," said Sam.

Robert just shrugged when Sam told him the plan. He was acting as if he didn't care, but Sam knew he was hurting.

BOTTLING
IT ALL UP INSIDE

As they passed Weird Science on the way to the veterinarian's office, Sam saw that the store was closed. He tried to remember if it was always closed on Sundays. Sam paused to peer in the window. Everything was dark.

Mabel wrinkled up her nose. "Mom and Dad took me there once. It smelled. It's weird."

"It's supposed to be weird," said Sam. "That's why it's called Weird Science. You wouldn't know a cool store if it fell on you."

"Oh, and you would?" asked Mabel. "That's why you look like you pick your clothes from a Dumpster."

"Could you two stop arguing so we can keep going to the vet's?" Robert marched ahead angrily.

Mabel and Sam looked at each other.

"Anger," whispered Mabel. "He's moving through the stages of grief." They hurried on.

When they got to the vet's office, Dr. Simon said that he was truly sorry. "We did what we could," he said. "He just died in his sleep."

"May I see him?" asked Robert.

Dr. Simon nodded. He disappeared into a back room and came out carrying a little cage. "He looks quite peaceful."

They all looked at the limp body lying on the bottom of the cage.

Robert turned away from the cage first. "Okay," he said. "Let's go."

"We have to wait for Mom. She's meeting us here," said Sam.

"Don't you want to say a few last words to him, Robert?" asked Mabel.

"No," said Robert through tight lips. "Let's get out of here."

"He's in denial," Mabel whispered to

Sam. "We have to help him move on to the next stage." She turned to Dr. Simon. "What happens to the remains?"

"We'll dispose of him," said Dr. Simon, softly. "Unless you want the body, Robert. There are pet burial services I can get you in touch with."

"Flush him down the toilet, stick him in the compactor," said Robert crossly. "It's just like Sam said yesterday. Who cares what happens to him!"

"I didn't mean all those things I said," said Sam. He felt terrible.

"Make some more jokes, why don't you?" snapped Robert. "He's gone to the Big Exterminator in the Sky. Maybe he'll meet some other rodents and have an exterminating party on the roof."

"Take it easy, Robert," said Willie. "We're sorry about that roof business."

"Well, it's all a big gag anyhow!" yelled Robert.

Mabel patted Robert on the back. "You're in pain right now. And that's okay." She murmured to Sam and Willie. "He was bottling

6

SOMETHING FOR NOTHING—IS THAT WEIRD OR WHAT?

"I didn't forget my MetroCard," said Sam to Willie. "I want to get Extermie's body."

"Why?" asked Willie. "What do you want with his body?"

"I've got an idea of how I can make it up to Robert," Sam explained. "You'll see."

They went back to the veterinarian's office. "Hi, Dr. Simon," said Sam. "My brother changed his mind. Can I have Exterminator's body? We're going to give him a proper burial."

"I'll put him on ice for you," said Dr. Simon.

"Sounds like a piece of fish," joked Willie.

everything up inside. He was bound to explode."

Sam looked at Extermie's limp body in the cage. His black-and-white fur still looked clean and fluffy. Sam remembered how much Extermie had loved to eat Rice Krispies, and all the times he had helped Robert feed him.

Just then Mrs. Bamford came running into the vet's office. She looked at Extermie and then at Robert.

"Oh, sweetie," she said. She gave him a hug.

Robert shrugged. "He's dead. But I don't care. He's just a rodent."

"But he was your rodent and you loved him," said Mrs. Bamford softly.

Robert just shrugged again.

"I've been telling him not to bottle up his sorrow," said Mabel. "But he won't cry."

"Will you all shut up?" Robert said. "Mom, I want to go home."

"I think it's something Sam said," said Mabel unhelpfully. "He and Willie made jokes, and now Robert can't grieve. It's very bad for him."

"Mabel, dear," said Mrs. Bamford, "I'm sure Sam didn't make jokes at a time like this."

"Yes, he did!" said Robert. "He said the gerbil was on the roof. It wasn't funny."

Mrs. Bamford looked aghast. "The gerbil is on the roof?"

"Sam was just repeating a joke I told him," said Willie.

"See," said Mabel. "I told you he was joking."

"Sam," said Mrs. Bamford, looking a little ashamed of him. "I know that joke. You didn't tell Robert that, did you?"

"Not exactly," said Sam. "See, Willie told it to me, and we were trying to think of how to tell Robert. And then he came into the room, and then I just blurted that roof stuff out."

Robert glared at his brother. "Sam makes a joke out of everything."

"I know," said Mabel sympathetically, taking Robert's hand.

"Come on, honey," said Mrs. Bamford, taking Robert by the other hand and giving Sam a look. "We'll go home now." Sam's shoulders drooped.

They walked out of the vet's office. Robert wouldn't even talk to Sam. They had gone half a block when they passed Weird Science. It was open now.

Suddenly Sam got an idea. "Mom," he said. "I think I forgot my MetroCard at the vet's. I'm going back to get it."

"Okay," said Mrs. Bamford. "Willie, why don't you go with Sam? Mabel and I will take Robert home. It's been a trying day for him."

everything up inside. He was bound to explode."

Sam looked at Extermie's limp body in the cage. His black-and-white fur still looked clean and fluffy. Sam remembered how much Extermie had loved to eat Rice Krispies, and all the times he had helped Robert feed him.

Just then Mrs. Bamford came running into the vet's office. She looked at Extermie and then at Robert.

"Oh, sweetie," she said. She gave him a hug.

Robert shrugged. "He's dead. But I don't care. He's just a rodent."

"But he was your rodent and you loved him," said Mrs. Bamford softly.

Robert just shrugged again.

"I've been telling him not to bottle up his sorrow," said Mabel. "But he won't cry."

"Will you all shut up?" Robert said. "Mom, I want to go home."

"I think it's something Sam said," said Mabel unhelpfully. "He and Willie made jokes, and now Robert can't grieve. It's very bad for him."

"Mabel, dear," said Mrs. Bamford, "I'm sure Sam didn't make jokes at a time like this."

"Yes, he did!" said Robert. "He said the gerbil was on the roof. It wasn't funny."

Mrs. Bamford looked aghast. "The gerbil is on the roof?"

"Sam was just repeating a joke I told him," said Willie.

"See," said Mabel. "I told you he was joking."

"Sam," said Mrs. Bamford, looking a little ashamed of him. "I know that joke. You didn't tell Robert that, did you?"

"Not exactly," said Sam. "See, Willie told it to me, and we were trying to think of how to tell Robert. And then he came into the room, and then I just blurted that roof stuff out."

Robert glared at his brother. "Sam makes a joke out of everything."

"I know," said Mabel sympathetically, taking Robert's hand.

"Come on, honey," said Mrs. Bamford, taking Robert by the other hand and giving

Sam a look. "We'll go home now." Sam's shoulders drooped.

They walked out of the vet's office. Robert wouldn't even talk to Sam. They had gone half a block when they passed Weird Science. It was open now.

Suddenly Sam got an idea. "Mom," he said. "I think I forgot my MetroCard at the vet's. I'm going back to get it."

"Okay," said Mrs. Bamford. "Willie, why don't you go with Sam? Mabel and I will take Robert home. It's been a trying day for him."

6

SOMETHING FOR NOTHING—IS THAT WEIRD OR WHAT?

"I didn't forget my MetroCard," said Sam to Willie. "I want to get Extermie's body."

"Why?" asked Willie. "What do you want with his body?"

"I've got an idea of how I can make it up to Robert," Sam explained. "You'll see."

They went back to the veterinarian's office. "Hi, Dr. Simon," said Sam. "My brother changed his mind. Can I have Exterminator's body? We're going to give him a proper burial."

"I'll put him on ice for you," said Dr. Simon.

"Sounds like a piece of fish," joked Willie.

A few minutes later, Dr. Simon came back with a little blue-and-white Styrofoam cooler that looked very much like the kind Mrs. Bamford packed for picnics in the park. He handed the box to Sam. Sam had a feeling that he would never look at a picnic cooler in quite the same way again.

"Man, I hope you know what you're doing," said Willie. "This seems a little weird to me."

"If you think this is weird, wait till you see where we're going," said Sam. He led Willie down the street to Weird Science.

The elephant bellow sounded as the door closed behind them. Sam wrinkled his nose. There was a very strange moldy odor coming from the store, kind of like seaweed that had been left in the sun too long.

Mr. Winston looked surprised to see Sam and Willie. "Oh, hello, Sam. I was a little late opening today. I wasn't expecting anybody so soon."

"It's an emergency, Mr. Winston," said Sam. He put the cooler on the counter. Mr. Winston seemed a little distracted. Hairs were straggling out of his long ponytail. He had a smudge on the left lens of his glasses.

"What kind of emergency?" asked Mr. Winston. "And who's your friend?"

"This is my neighbor Willie." Sam noticed that the moldy seaweedy smell was actually coming from Mr. Winston. He wanted to hold his nose, but he didn't want to be rude.

Willie looked around at all the fossils and snake skeletons. "This place is cool," he said.

"Thank you, Willie. May I ask what you have in that cooler?"

"It's Robert's gerbil," said Sam. "He's dead."

"Oh, yes . . . I know . . . ," said Mr. Winston solemnly.

"How did you know?" Sam asked, astonished. "It just happened."

Mr. Winston coughed. "I meant to say that I know that the death of a family pet can be tough on you—and the whole family."

"It's Robert I'm worried about," said Sam. "He's acting like he doesn't care, but I know he does. And I made a bunch of stupid jokes when Extermie got sick . . . so I was thinking . . . I mean, he just died. . . ." Sam was stammering. This was much harder to get out than he had imagined.

Mr. Winston peered at Sam over his smudged glasses. "You were thinking of a living memorial."

"Well, not exactly," said Sam. "He's dead."

"I can make him live again," said Mr. Winston, his eyes gleaming. He opened the cooler and looked in. "Ahh," he said. "Satisfactory." He closed the top of the cooler. "Now, tell me about the deceased."

A cloud covered the sun, and suddenly the store was thrown into shadow. Sam had never noticed how dark the store got on a cloudy day. He found himself staring into the glassy eye of an African kudu on the wall as he tried to avoid Mr. Winston's intense gaze.

"Tell me *everything* about the little warrior in the cooler," said Mr. Winston.

"The little what?" exclaimed Sam.

"The little warrior," said Mr. Winston. "The gerbil."

Sam was not sure that he would ever have called Extermie a "little warrior."

"He was a good chewer. Mostly he just chewed on the paper towels on the bottom of his cage," said Sam. "Why did you call him 'the little warrior'?"

"The species name for *gerbil* is *gerbillus*, but the scientific name for this kind of gerbil is *Meriones unguiculatus*," said Mr. Winston. "It's Latin for 'Mongolian warrior.' Gerbils come from a long line of warrior-like animals. And intelligent ones, at that."

"Well, Exterminator could stand on his back feet. I guess that took intelligence," said Sam.

"Exterminator," repeated Mr. Winston. "I remember now. That was his name." He wrote it down on a little pad.

"Robert named his gerbils Terminator and Exterminator," said Sam. "Terminator is still alive."

"Those are very good names for gerbils," said Mr. Winston. "Your brother had good instincts."

Sam thought of Robert's sad, tight face when he had turned away from Exterminator's body at the vet's. He hoped he was doing the right thing.

"Anything else you can tell me about the gerbil in the cooler?" asked Mr. Winston.

"Well, as I said, he was great at chewing and standing on his back feet."

"Then that's the pose we'll use. You see, each animal has its own personality—and my job is to show that. Do you want to come see my workshop in the back?"

"Sure," said Willie, a little too quickly for Sam's taste.

Mr. Winston picked up the cooler and led Sam and Willie into the back room. The smell was even stronger, almost overpowering. The first thing Sam saw was a big basket of eyes staring at him. Bit and pieces of what looked like bones were scattered everywhere. A giant python snakeskin was lying on the bench.

"You can touch the snakeskin if you want," said Mr. Winston.

Sam reached out and touched the snakeskin gingerly. It felt extremely dry.

"Extermie isn't going to dry out, is he?" asked Sam. He was trying to keep his mind off how spooky the workroom was.

"Oh no!" said Mr. Winston. "I take care so that my creations last a long time. He'll look just like he did when he was alive."

Sam stared at him. After all, Extermie *was* dead.

"How do you . . . you know . . . stuff him?" asked Willie.

"I'm glad you asked, young man." Mr. Winston rubbed his hands together. He placed them on top of the cooler.

"First, I make a little incision in his stomach. Then I pull off his skin, making sure to keep it intact. It's just like taking a little person out of a suit of clothes. Then I pour in a strong chemical called Borax that gets rid of the inner body parts—the guts, the stomach, the muscles. They would smell if they were left in. Then I look for the perfect glass eye."

Sam's own stomach was beginning to churn. He was learning a lot more about what was going to happen to Extermie's body than he wanted to. Besides, all those steps made it sound very expensive. "Uh . . . how much is this going to cost?" Sam asked, beginning to worry.

"Well, Sam," said Mr. Winston. "Because I just moved here from Pennsylvania and you come from such a nice family and were one of my first customers, I'll do it for free. How does that sound?"

"For free?" Sam could hardly believe it. "Wow, thank you!" Mr. Winston was a nice man after all, even if he was a little too much into his job.

"It might take a few days," Mr. Winston added. "I have the possibility of a big job coming in from the museum this week. But I'll get started right away."

"Whenever," said Sam quickly. He didn't want to stick around to see what was going to happen to Extermie. "Thanks, Mr. Winston. Good-bye!"

Sam and Willie were both quiet on the way to the subway. Then Willie turned to Sam. "It's weird that he'd do all that work for free. I don't know many shops in New York that would do *anything* for free."

"Well, Mr. Winston's not from New

York," mused Sam. "He said he just moved here from Pennsylvania."

"Usually, when something's free, it means there's a string attached," said Willie.

"A string attached?" asked Sam. "What does that mean?"

"He might want something in return. Maybe he's got an ulterior motive."

"Like what?" Sam demanded.

Willie shrugged. "I don't know. He just reminded me of someone, but I can't remember who. I'll tell you this, though. He's as weird as his store."

On the subway, Sam wondered exactly what an ulterior motive was. It didn't sound very good. Still, it would all be worth it if getting Extermie stuffed helped Robert get over Extermie's death.

Just as they got to the apartment door, Willie snapped his fingers. "I got it! Mr. Winston looked just like that guy in the movie I was telling you about—the zombie."

7

WAS THAT PENNSYLVANIA OR TRANSYLVANIA?

All that week, Sam worried about Robert. He just seemed so down in the dumps. So, on Monday morning, as they were getting ready for school, Sam let himself into Robert's room.

"How are you doing, bro?" he asked.

Robert didn't answer. He just shrugged and went on putting on his clothes. Behind him, on the top of his desk, Terminator was furiously running on his wheel. But Robert wasn't even giving Termie the time of day.

Sam looked down at Terminator.

"Do you think he misses his buddy?"

Robert shrugged again. Sam noticed that Robert was shrugging a lot lately.

"I don't know what gerbils feel," muttered Robert. "After all, they're just rodents."

"Yeah, but they're rodents with personality. I think Exterminator had a real warrior personality. I miss him. I bet you and Termie do too."

"I can't tell if Terminator misses Exterminator or not," snapped Robert. "He's probably forgotten all about him. Maybe that's the way things should be. Just forget about someone or something after it's gone."

"I don't think that's a good idea," said Sam. "I think it's good to keep the memory of someone alive. Then it's like they live forever—I mean it doesn't mean that they're not dead, but . . ."

"You know, I don't like it when you sound like Mabel," barked Robert. He stormed out of the room.

Sam realized he did sound a little like Mabel. It was scary.

Later that day at school, Mabel stopped Sam in the hall. "You know, I've been thinking."

"That's always dangerous," said Sam.

"No, seriously," said Mabel. Nothing could stop her. "I think we made a mistake."

"We?" Sam didn't like the sound of that. He tried to think of what he had done lately that could be a mistake. Sam made lots of mistakes, sometimes too many to keep track of.

"What kind of mistake?" he asked suspiciously.

"We should have *made* Robert have a memorial service—or done *something* to help him get over Extermie's death. We need to help him bring closure to his grief."

"What's closure?" Even though Mabel was two years younger than Sam, she often used words that Sam didn't know.

"It's a way of coming to terms with"— Mabel lowered her voice—"death. People need a way to express their grief. That's why the Egyptians built the pyramids."

"I don't think we can build a pyramid for Exterminator," said Sam. He brightened.

"But I've done something better—something that will cheer Robert up."

"You wrote a poem about Extermie! 'Ode to a Gerbil Dying Young,'" gushed Mabel.

"It's better than that," bragged Sam. "It's a living memorial."

Mabel looked puzzled. "You're starting a fund for homeless gerbils in Extermie's name?" she guessed. "That's a good idea. Although, I must say, I didn't realize that there was a homeless gerbil problem."

"It's way better than that!" said Sam, getting impatient. Finally, he couldn't keep it to himself anymore. "I'm having Extermie stuffed."

Mabel stared at him. "Excuse me?"

"Yes," said Sam proudly. "I'm going to see if he's ready today after school. It's been a week."

"You had him stuffed?" repeated Mabel.

"By an expert!" bragged Sam. "Mr. Winston at Weird Science."

"This I've got to see," said Mabel.

"You can come with me, but don't tell Robert. I want it to be a surprise."

After school, Sam and Mabel walked over to Weird Science. Mabel held her nose at the odor in the store. Sam wished that he hadn't brought her.

"Sam, I ran into a little problem," said Mr. Winston. He looked tired. There were circles under his eyes.

"A problem?" said Sam anxiously.

"Well, I got a rush job from the Museum of Natural History. So I had to send your brother's gerbil to my brother in Pennsylvania."

"Pennsylvania," exclaimed Mabel. "Exterminator's in Pennsylvania?"

"No, he's back. I sent him on dry ice by express mail. And my brother shipped him back to me just today. We send projects to each other all the time. I'm just sorry I couldn't do it myself, Sam."

"May I see him?" Sam asked.

Mr. Winston brought out the cooler. "He's wrapped in bubble wrap," he said. "My brother does a terrific job of packing."

Sam opened the cooler and peered in cautiously.

"I think you should let Robert be the first to unwrap him," said Mabel. "It could be an important step for him in the healing process."

"Excuse me?" asked Mr. Winston.

"She always talks that way," said Sam. "But maybe she's right. I think I will let Robert unwrap him."

Mabel put her hand on the cooler. "I think this will help Robert come to acceptance," she said. "The grieving one must realize that life goes on. This could be the centerpiece of a memorial service."

"I would very much like to be there," said Mr. Winston. He looked intently at Sam through his glasses. "What time is the service?"

Sam couldn't get any words out. The shop and Mr. Winston were beginning to get to him—the smell, the glass eyes everywhere. Sam suddenly remembered what Willie had said about Mr. Winston looking like a zombie from that movie, *Night of the Living Dead.* Mr. Winston *did* look extremely pale today. Maybe it wouldn't be a good idea to have Mr. Winston at the service.

"Uh . . . well, I think it'll be small—and we haven't scheduled it yet," Sam said quickly. He was anxious to get out of there. "'Bye, Mr. Winston. Thanks again!"

Sam picked up the cooler, grabbed Mabel, and hustled out the door. The elephant bellowed behind him. It almost sounded like it was laughing at him.

"There's something very peculiar about that man," said Mabel.

Sam struggled to get a better grip on the cooler. "I don't want to hear about it," he muttered.

Naturally that didn't affect Mabel a bit. "Don't you think it's strange that Mr. Winston sent Extermie to Pennsylvania? You do realize that 'Pennsylvania' rhymes with 'Transylvania.' Transylvania—the home of Dracula?"

"So what?" muttered Sam, wishing more than ever that he hadn't invited Mabel to come along. "It's probably just a coincidence."

"I wonder why Mr. Winston wanted to come to the service," mused Mabel.

"Could you just keep quiet," pleaded Sam.

Mabel looked from Sam to the cooler. "Of course. After all, you are carrying the dead body. This is a solemn moment."

Sam grunted. He didn't want to worry Mabel, but he was beginning to think that there was something creepy about the fact that Mr. Winston seemed to be taking such a personal interest in the entire Bamford family. Even those members like Extermie, who were dead. Maybe he even had a *special* interest in the dead ones.

8

THE NIGHT OF THE LIVING EYEBALL

It was a dark and stormy afternoon. The storm broke just as Sam got home from Mr. Winston's. He took the cooler into his room. Sam really wanted to see what Extermie looked like, but he *had* promised Mabel that he would let Robert unwrap it. So he put the cooler with the bubble-wrapped Extermie in the back of his closet and closed the door. Just then, he heard his mother calling him.

When Sam went into the living room, Mrs. Bamford was talking to Robert. She was all dressed up. "Hi, honey. I'm going out tonight, but Willie is coming down to baby-sit for you."

"You've been going out a lot lately," complained Robert. "Ever since Extermie died."

"Speaking of Extermie," said Sam, "Mabel and I were thinking that we should have a memorial service for him. You know, where we each talk about him."

"That sounds nice," said Mrs. Bamford. "Robert, dear, what do you think?"

Robert shrugged. Sam rolled his eyes at his mother. He thought that if his brother shrugged one more time he might punch him.

"Maybe a memorial service is exactly what we need," said Mrs. Bamford. "How about tomorrow night? We could order take-out Chinese. I'll invite Mabel and her parents."

Robert shrugged his shoulders again.

"Come on, sweetheart," said Mrs. Bamford. "I know you've been sad ever since Extermie died. Sam's idea just might cheer you up."

Sam felt a little smug. If Mom thought the memorial service idea was good, wait until she found out what he, Sam, had done for his brother. For once, he was doing something for Robert that was even nicer than anybody else, and his mom didn't even know about it. The memorial service would be the perfect place for the unveiling of the living monument.

Just then there was a tremendous clap of thunder. Mrs. Bamford went to the closet and got her umbrella.

"Are you really going out in this storm?" Robert asked.

"Oh, I like a little electricity in the air," said Mrs. Bamford with a smile. "It makes you feel alive."

Sam and Robert looked at each other. She'd been acting kind of strange lately.

"Wow! What a storm!" said Willie when he came in a few minutes later.

A bolt of lightning flashed across the sky, illuminating the trees of Central Park outside the window.

"It's not a fit night out for man or beast," he continued in his scary voice. "The kind of night where you can't tell the living from the dead!" Willie laughed evilly. Then he pulled his eyelid out from his eyeball.

"Eewww!" said Robert. "What are you doing?"

"I'm one of the living dead!" Willie flipped his eyelid over his eyeball.

Robert screamed. Sam tried to giggle, but it came out more like a gurgle.

Willie flipped his other eyeball and began walking around the room like a zombie. "You know that movie I was telling you about, *Night of the Living Dead*? Well, maybe it wasn't just a movie!" He headed toward Sam and Robert with his arms stiff in front of him.

Sam and Robert ran into Sam's room and hid in the closet. They knew Willie was probably joking, but they didn't want to take any chances, especially on a night like tonight.

Willie laughed. "Only kidding, guys," he said. "Listen, I've got some homework to do. Leave me alone for a while, okay?"

Robert sank to the floor of the closet and let out a relieved sigh. Suddenly there was a thump. Robert jumped up. "What's that!" he yelped.

Sam was horrified to see that Robert had knocked over the cooler and the bubble-wrapped package had fallen out.

Pop! Pop! Pop! It sounded as if firecrackers were going off in the closet. Or as if something were alive in the closet with them.

"What's that!" Robert demanded. He picked up the bubble-wrapped package and ran out of the closet.

"Give me that!" demanded Sam, trying to grab the package. "It's a surprise!"

"I want to see!" said Robert, holding on to it. He took it over to the window. Just then there was another flash of lightning.

Sam reached out and grabbed a loose end of the bubble wrap. It popped in his hand. Then the bubble wrap began to unravel.

The outline of a gerbil's body became clear. His back feet were glued to a block of wood. His front claws were curled as if he was ready to attack. His mouth was open, showing his sharp teeth.

"EXTERMINATOR!" shrieked Robert. "He's back from the dead!"

This wasn't exactly the healing moment that Sam had been hoping for.

Willie knocked on the door. "Is anything wrong?"

Robert was shaking.

"No, we're okay," said Sam quickly.

"Good," said Willie. "This is some storm. It's enough to wake the dead." Willie went back to his homework.

"Robert," Sam whispered urgently. "Extermie's not really alive! I had him stuffed. Mr. Winston at Weird Science did it for me."

"Mr. Winston at that weird smelly store?" hissed Robert. He looked down at his stuffed pet. It looked like Extermie, but Extermie had never looked so fierce. "I think he moved! Just a little. Mr. Winston probably turned him into a zombie—just like that movie Willie told us about."

"I don't think he's a zombie," Sam said. But the more he looked at Exterminator, the scarier he looked. Sam had never imagined that Exterminator would come back looking so angry, with his little fangs bared. Maybe Robert was right. Maybe he *had* moved.

"You took my dead gerbil to a zombie-maker," accused Robert.

"I thought it would make you feel better," said Sam.

Just then another lightning bolt lit up the

sky, throwing the outline of Extermie's body against the wall.

"He scares me!" said Robert.

Sam was a little scared too. But he didn't want Robert to know that. "Why don't you keep him in your room?" he suggested.

"Put him in *my* room! Are you kidding!" yelped Robert. "He'll probably take a bite out of Termie and turn him into a living dead gerbil too."

Sam looked at the ferocious creature in Robert's hand. "Let's rewrap him and put him away for now," he said. "Tomorrow at the memorial service, we can figure out what to do with him."

Sam wound the bubble wrap around Exterminator. He put the package back in the cooler and put the whole thing in the back of his closet. Then he closed the door firmly.

"Maybe you should sleep in my room tonight," said Robert.

"Good idea," said Sam.

9

THE HORROR!
THE HORROR!

The next day neither Sam nor Robert went near the closet all day. They were trying to pretend that a stuffed, dead—but possibly *living* dead—creature wasn't lurking inside their home.

Right before dinner, Mabel and her parents came over for Extermie's memorial service. Mabel was dressed in black from head to toe. She carried a wreath she had made herself out of paper tissues. She had dyed the tissues black. She had made a banner with the words "Exterminator—He's Not Exterminated From Our Hearts" printed on it and strung it across the wreath.

"That's a big wreath for a little gerbil," said Mrs. Bamford.

"He's not little in our hearts," said Mabel.

Mabel's parents nodded proudly. Sam rolled his eyes.

"Robert," said Mabel in her most solemn voice. "I'm glad we could be together for this day."

"I only hope we live through today," said Robert. He couldn't help thinking that Extermie was skulking in the closet, maybe angry because he was dead.

"Oh, no," said Mabel. "You're regressing. According to the stages of grief, you should be beyond depression by now."

"I'm not depressed," muttered Robert. "I'm scared. A dead gerbil out for revenge is not a pretty sight."

Mabel looked from Sam to Robert. "What's going on?" she asked.

Just then there was a knock at the door. Mr. Winston came in. "Hello everyone. I hope I'm not late."

Mrs. Bamford greeted him warmly. "Hi, Ben!"

Robert's mouth dropped open. "What's he doing here?" he whispered to Sam and Mabel.

"I don't know!" said Sam. He sounded panicky. "He wanted to come, but I'm sure that I didn't tell him when it would be. How did he find out?"

"He must be a zombie himself," whispered Robert. "Zombies probably know when a memorial service is going on. Maybe they can smell death."

"Kids," said Mrs. Bamford. "Come say hello to Ben."

Mr. Winston held his hand out to Sam. Sam noticed that Mr. Winston looked paler than ever. And the circles under his eyes were even darker.

Robert hid behind Sam. "Don't shake his hand," he whispered into Sam's ear. "If you touch him you might turn into a zombie."

"What's wrong, Sam?" asked Mr. Winston. "You look pale, like you've seen a ghost." He leaned down toward Sam.

Sam got a slight whiff of the odor from the store. Now he knew what that odor was. Zombie odor.

"Sam," said Mrs. Bamford, "I understand you did something very nice for Robert." She smiled at Sam. "I'm excited to see it. Where is it?"

"Uh . . . in my closet," stammered Sam. "But . . . but . . ."

"It's time to begin the ceremony," Mabel interrupted. "Sam, why don't you bring out the living memorial."

Sam didn't know what to do. He knew the adults wouldn't believe him if he told them that Extermie might be a zombie. There just didn't seem to be any way out.

Sam went into the bedroom, brought out the creature wrapped in bubble wrap, and handed it to Mabel. Then he braced himself.

Mabel straightened her shoulders. She loved to be the center of attention. "We are gathered here today to honor Exterminator," she intoned. "Robert, since you are the bereaved, I think you should have the seat of honor."

"What seat of honor?" asked Robert. He wanted this service to be over pronto so he could get that lurking zombie gerbil back in the closet, where it belonged.

"I think you should sit in that chair by the window," said Mabel. "The window will bring healing sunlight. Sam, as the brother of the bereaved, you can stand next to him."

"How long is this going to take?" asked Sam, casting nervous looks at Mr. Winston.

Mabel ignored Sam's question and went back to the center of the room. "Dearly beloved, we have gathered together to remember Exterminator, an extraordinary, exuberant, extravagant, extra-special gerbil."

"What did she do, go through the dictionary and look for words that begin with 'x'?" Robert whispered to Sam.

"That's exactly the kind of thing that she would do," said Sam.

Mabel looked annoyed that the bereaved were not paying complete attention to her. She turned to Robert. "Do you want to bring in the other bereaved party?"

"The what?" asked Robert.

Mrs. Bamford put her arm around Robert's shoulder. "Mabel, dear, Robert *is* the bereaved party. I think we should just go on with the ceremony. We do want to have dinner."

Mabel looked put out. "I meant Terminator, the living relative. Terminator should be here."

"She's not going to quit until everything is exactly the way she wants it," warned Sam. "Better get him."

"If I bring Terminator out here, what if he turns into a zombie," hissed Robert.

"We'll be careful," whispered Sam. "Besides, we should try to act normal. We don't want Mr. Winston to suspect that we're on to him."

Robert nodded. That made sense. He went into his room and brought out Terminator in his cage. He put the cage down on the windowsill and sat back in his chair.

"Robert," said Mabel. "Perhaps you should be the one to speak for Terminator and tell us what he is feeling."

"I don't think so," said Robert. "Terminator doesn't talk. He just chews."

Mr. Winston coughed. "Sam, perhaps now would be a good time to make *your* presentation."

Sam gingerly picked up the bubble-wrapped package and handed it to Robert.

Robert's hands began to shake.

Mabel stepped forward. "Ah, is the grief too much for you? Let me help."

"Don't!" warned Sam and Robert together.

It was too late. Mabel grabbed the package and started to unwrap it. She removed the last layer of bubble wrap and found herself face-to-face with a fierce little creature with glassy eyes and bared teeth. Mabel screamed and flung the stuffed gerbil into the air. By some instinct Robert managed to catch the flying gerbil.

Sam could only blink—his mouth dropping open.

"Oh, the horror! The horror!" screamed Mabel. Stumbling backward, she bumped into Terminator's cage, which flew out the window. Sam's mouth clamped shut. He couldn't believe that things could get worse. But they just had.

10

IS TERMINATOR TERMINATED?

The entire memorial party ran to the window and looked down. Terminator's cage was lying on top of the canopy over the doorway to the apartment building. There was no way of knowing whether Terminator was alive or dead.

Everybody ran into the hallway and frantically pushed the button for the elevator. Robert clutched the stuffed version of Exterminator to his chest without realizing what he was doing.

The elevator seemed to take forever. When it finally came they all piled in. They ran outside. The doorman was looking up at

74

the canopy with an alarmed expression on his face. "What was that?" he asked.

Without a word, Mr. Winston shimmied up the pole that held the canopy above the sidewalk. When he got to the top, he held onto the pole with one hand and reached for the cage with the other.

"Ben, be careful," shouted Mrs. Bamford.

After a moment, Mr. Winston jumped to the ground, cage safely in hand. Terminator was lying on the bottom of it, not moving.

"He's dead too, isn't he?" sobbed Robert.

"Let's get him inside," said Mr. Winston. He looked even paler than before.

Back in the Bamfords' apartment, Mr. Winston gently took Terminator out of his cage. He pressed on his little rib cage, once, twice, three times. Terminator's chest heaved up and down.

"Oh, Ben!" sighed Mrs. Bamford. "He's alive!" She threw her arms around Mr. Winston and planted a kiss on his lips.

"Aaagh!!! My mom kissed a zombie!" shrieked Robert. He grabbed Terminator and ran out of the room. Exterminator, stuffed

and silent, was clutched under his other arm. Sam and Mabel dashed after him.

"Children!" yelled Mrs. Bamford.

Sam, Robert, and Mabel got safely to Robert's room and slammed the door. Robert trembled as he looked from the stuffed Exterminator, caught permanently in an attack position, to the back-from-the-dead Terminator.

"Quick!" said Sam. "Let's barricade ourselves in here. Help me push the desk against the door."

Mabel and Robert helped Sam push the desk against the door.

"Why are we doing this?" Mabel demanded, out of breath.

"We don't know who's alive and who's dead," whispered Robert. He stared down at Terminator. Terminator twitched his nose. Then he calmly chewed on a piece of lettuce. He seemed amazingly recovered from his fall.

"Terminator could be one of the living dead," Sam explained to Mabel. "He may be a zombie like Willie told us about from

Night of the Living Dead."

"When Sam got Mr. Winston to stuff Exterminator he turned real life into Night of the Living Gerbil," said Robert, as if that would make everything clear.

Mabel picked up Exterminator. She didn't believe in zombies. "I think Mr. Winston likes your mother," she said casually.

"Eewwww," said Robert and Sam together.

Just then there was a banging on the door. "Robert, Sam, Mabel! Come out of there and explain yourselves," demanded Mrs. Bamford.

"No!" said Robert. "There's a zombie out there."

"What!" said Mrs. Bamford.

"It's my fault," said Sam. "Mr. Winston turned Exterminator into a zombie. He's probably one too!"

"Open the door this instant!" yelled Mrs. Bamford. "I mean it."

Sam and Robert glanced at each other. There was only one thing scarier than a zombie—and that was their mom when she sounded as angry as she did at that moment.

They knew they had no choice. They opened the door.

11

A COOL ZOMBIE

Mrs. Bamford stood in the hall with her hands on her hips. Mr. Winston was right behind her.

"Exactly what has gotten into you children!" demanded Mrs. Bamford. "I've never seen you act so rudely. And after Ben saved Terminator's life, too. You owe him an apology—big time!"

Sam and Robert hesitated. It was hard to apologize to a zombie.

Mrs. Bamford glared at them. Sam and Robert could tell she was really angry. "I'm sorry, Mr. Winston," they said together.

Mr. Winston had a puzzled expression on his face. "I just don't understand. You never seemed afraid of me before. Why now?"

Sam and Robert looked at the floor.

"Sam, Robert," warned Mrs. Bamford. "We're waiting for an explanation."

Sam stepped forward. He was responsible. It had been his idea to get Exterminator stuffed.

"Well, you see, Mr. Winston," he began. "Willie told us about this movie, *Night of the Living Dead*. It's about people who pretend to be alive, only they're not. They're zombies. Then, when you said that you'd stuff Extermie for free, it seemed weird. And your store smells funny. Then Exterminator came back looking scary. And he looked so alive— we even thought we saw him move. And you knew when we were having the memorial service even though we didn't tell you what time. You have big dark circles under your eyes, kind of like a zombie. And just now, you brought Terminator back from the dead. Does this make any sense?"

"No," said Mrs. Bamford.

But Mr. Winston nodded. "It makes sense to me," he said.

Sam's eyes widened. "It does?"

81

"Sam and Robert, I'm sorry that I scared you," said Mr. Winston. "But you've got to remember that *Night of the Living Dead* is just a movie. There's really no such thing as a zombie. I'm sure your gerbil didn't really move after he was stuffed. Sometimes your imagination just plays tricks on you."

"Still, what about the zombie smells?" asked Robert. "And the circles under your eyes. And why does Extermie look so scary?"

"Robert, sweetie," said Mrs. Bamford. "Those aren't exactly nice questions."

"It's okay," said Mr. Winston. "It's good to get all your suspicions out in the open. The shop smells because of the chemicals I use in my work. I've got circles under my eyes because I've been up late almost every night, working on a job for the museum. As for why Exterminator came out looking so fierce—well, I guess I have to blame my brother. When he heard that I was sending him a gerbil named Exterminator, he probably thought that the owner would want to remember the gerbil as the warrior that gerbils were originally named after. Robert, does

it really bother you to see him like that?"

Robert looked at Extermie. "No," he said finally. "I think he would have liked looking like this—kind of like a cool zombie."

"Not a zombie," corrected Mr. Winston. "Your brother wanted you to have a loving re-creation of a pet that passed away. He cared that you were sad."

"Thank you, Sam," said Robert. He put Extermie on the night table by his bed. "I guess it's not the night of the living gerbil after all."

"No, definitely not!" said Mrs. Bamford. "But it is a great night for good friends and family to get together." She smiled at Mr. Winston. "Ben is going to be doing a science program at your school. We'll all be seeing a lot of one another."

Sam and Robert looked at each other. This was going to take a lot of getting used to.